PRINCESS HORRID

Erik Christian Haugaard

ILLUSTRATED BY

Diane Dawson Hearn

Macmillan Publishing Company   New York

FOR MASAKO — E.C.H.

FOR LEANA AND MELANIE — D.D.H.

Macmillan Publishing Company, 866 Third Avenue, New York, NY 10022. Collier Macmillan Canada, Inc.

Printed and bound in Hong Kong   First American Edition   10   9   8   7   6   5   4   3   2   1

The text of this book is set in 14 point Bembo. The illustrations are rendered in pen and ink and acrylic wash.

Library of Congress Cataloging-in-Publication Data • Haugaard, Erik Christian. Princess Horrid/by Erik Christian
Haugaard; illustrated by Diane Dawson Hearn. — 1st American ed.   p.   cm.
Summary: Called Princess Horrid by everyone except her parents, a very badly behaved princess is transformed into
a kitten and becomes the property of the lowliest kitchen maid in the castle.
ISBN 0-02-743445-1
[1. Fairy tales. 2. Behavior — Fiction.] I. Hearn, Diane Dawson, ill. II. Title.
PZ8.H2934Ps   1990   [Fic] — dc20   89-8227   CIP   AC

ONCE upon a time in a kingdom by the sea there lived a princess so very bad that everyone—except her parents—called her Princess Horrid.

"She is mischievous," the Queen admitted. "Her father has spoiled her."

"She is full of devilment," the King allowed. "It is her mother's fault. She has indulged her too much."

"I am a princess!" said the Princess. "Need I say more?" And she didn't.

In the old times, thought the Prime Minister, there were dragons whose favorite meal was a princess. But the dragons have long been dead and gone, which is a great pity. He never said this aloud. It was because he did so much more thinking than speaking that he had become Prime Minister.

"She should be sent to bed without her supper," said one of the lowliest of all the scullery maids. She thought this was the worst punishment that could be given to anyone, for she was often hungry. But no one heard her, for no one thought her opinion worth listening to.

"The Princess is charming," said the Ladies-in-Waiting to the Queen, but they did not mean it.

"She is ever so intelligent," added a baroness who was Third Lady-in-Waiting to the Queen, although she suspected it was the Princess who had put a toad in her bed.

Too clever by half, thought the Chamberlain, who came from a family so old and aristocratic that he never spoke to anyone or even answered when spoken to. He was sure it was the Princess who had put a pin in the pillow of his favorite chair, the one he took a nap in after dinner.

"What is the point of being a princess if you have to be good?" asked the Princess as she made up an apple-pie bed for the First Lady of the Royal Bedchamber, who was also a Dowager Duchess.

The next morning the Dowager Duchess, who had three generals and an admiral among her ancestors, went to the Queen and complained about the apple-pie bed. "In my youth such pranks would have been considered worse than naughty. I want the culprit punished!"

"But that was a very long time ago. Times have changed," said the Queen, hiding a smile. "I shall look into it."

"I suspect the Princess," declared the Duchess. She was not afraid of anyone, not even the Queen. Then she made a curtsy, without bending her knees much, and left.

"She has no sense of humor," said the King. "Besides, she is so old that she can recall my grandfather as a young man. I wish she would retire."

"She won't," said the Queen, "because she can't get along with her daughter-in-law, the present Duchess."

"Fire her," suggested the King. "You don't need a First Lady of the Royal Bedchamber. I don't like her. My father didn't like her. Neither did my grandfather."

"You can't fire someone who has three generals and an admiral among her ancestors. It is an honorary position with no salary and no work attached to it. Besides, a queen who has no First Lady of the Royal Bedchamber is no queen at all."

"Then tell our daughter to make her an apple-pie bed every day until she leaves." The King grinned.

"I suppose she is a bit naughty even for a princess," the Queen admitted. She liked to be fair.

"She will outgrow it," declared the King, and yawned. He found conversations that were not about himself boring.

"I shall speak to her in the morning. But I wish you wouldn't spoil her so, my dear."

"Sons are for fighting, and daughters are for spoiling," said the King, taking off his golden crown.

"TIMES have changed.... Apple-pie beds!" snorted the Duchess as she made her way to her apartments in the East Tower.

"Take down my great-great-grandmother's book of magic and bring it to me!" she commanded in so frightening a tone that her little maid, whose name was Fetch-and-Carry, decided to run away the next day.

The book was very large and heavy. It was bound in batskin and had gold edges. At the sight of it the Duchess felt better. "In those times they knew what quality meant," she muttered, and put on her spectacles.

"Let me see…. Spells would be under *S,*" she said as she turned over the leaves of the book. "Here we are! Spells for Disobedient Servants." The Duchess glanced at her maid, who decided that she would run away as soon as she had had her supper. "Spells against Princes and Princesses. That's better. How to Turn Royal Personages into Toads"—the Duchess paused and then read on— "or into Spiders, Snakes, Lizards, Dogs, Donkeys, and Cats. Cats will do," she mumbled.

The recipe for the spell was even longer than the one in the Royal Cookbook for the King's Birthday Cake, and the ingredients weren't half as nice. But it could have been worse. The recipe for the Spell to Turn a Princess into a Toad called for nasty things like a teaspoon of snake spit and three deadly nightshade leaves gathered at midnight.

It was nearly morning before the Duchess had finished brewing her spell. She poured it into a bottle and labeled it *Sweet-tasting Medicine—must NOT be drunk by children.* Then she put it on the night table and got into bed. She was so tired that she slept until noon.

THE following day was a busy one for Princess Horrid. She put itching powder down the Chamberlain's back while he slept and dumped one of her father's old socks into the soup the cook was boiling for the Ladies-in-Waiting's lunch. Then she teased the Baroness's white poodle and gave it its owner's favorite satin slipper to chew to pieces.

It was late in the afternoon before she had time to make an apple-pie bed for the old Duchess. She sneaked into her bedroom. To tell the truth, the Duchess was the only person in the castle whom Princess Horrid was afraid of.

"What is that?" she exclaimed as soon as she saw the bottle on the bedside table. "*Sweet-tasting Medicine—must NOT be drunk by children…* I am not a child! I am a princess!" She uncorked the bottle and sniffed the contents. Whatever was in it smelled delicious, as if it had been brewed from all the candies that had ever existed in the world.

"A sip won't hurt." Princess Horrid took one; then, as one sip did not hurt, she took another and another until soon the bottle was empty.

"I think I am getting a tummy ache.... Oh, it hurts! I am sorry I ever drank that stupid medicine.... Oh, oh, mi, oh, mia-oh-miaow!" There she was, changed into a kitten, and all she could say was "Miaow!"

"A kitten in my bedroom!" The Duchess stepped out from where she had been watching behind the door. She grabbed Princess Horrid by the neck and held her up. Then she rang for her little maid, but the maid had long ago run away. Next she called the Royal Housekeeper, a very grand woman who kept all the keys of the castle hanging from her waist.

"Please remove this kitten!" the Duchess ordered, and handed the poor Princess to her.

"Please dispose of this kitten!" The Royal Housekeeper was too important a person to do anything more than order everybody

else about, so she handed Princess Horrid to the Royal Assistant Housekeeper, who carried the kitten as she would a speck of dirt found in the Royal Bedchamber. In this way Princess Horrid was handed from one servant to another until she ended up in the hands of a maid whose name was Pots-and-Pans. She was so lowly that she had no one to pass the kitten on to.

"What a darling kitten!" she said, and stroked Princess Horrid with her hands, which were all red and swollen from scrubbing.

"I am a princess!" mewed Princess Horrid, but she purred, for the scullery maid was the first person who had been nice to her.

"I wonder what your name is." Pots-and-Pans set the kitten on her lap.

"I am Princess Hyacinth," mewed the kitten. That was the name she had been given by her parents the day she was born.

"I shall call you Miaow, since that is all you can say."

No sooner had the maid spoken than Princess Horrid, who did not like her new name, put all her claws out.

"Ouch!" cried Pots-and-Pans. "I should call you Horrid, for you are a horrid little kitten!"

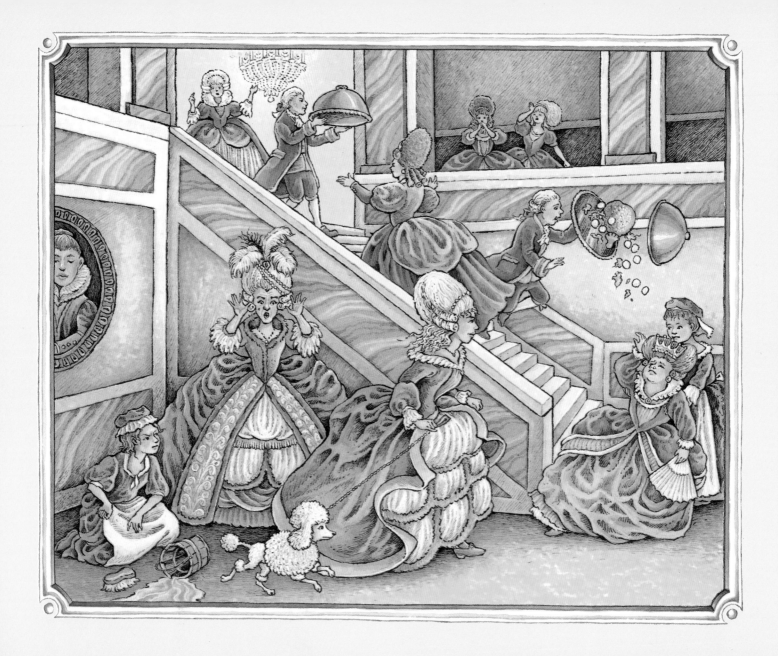

BY suppertime, when no one could find the Princess, a great search was made. The King himself bent his royal knees and looked under his bed. Although he did not find his daughter there, he felt he had done his duty. The Queen searched her closets and the Great Hall, which made her so tired that she had to go to bed early.

The Ladies-in-Waiting ran around the castle like frightened hens, causing a great disturbance but not accomplishing much. The Baroness, who had a name so long that no one—not even herself—knew how to spell it, climbed to the top of the Great Tower. But the other ladies said she had done it just to show off.

The next day the King proclaimed that anyone who found Princess Hyacinth would be given a barrel of gold and the title of Royal Princess Finder.

IN the closet under the stairs where she lived, the scullery maid took good care of her kitten. She fed her fish and cream, both of which she had gotten from the cook without asking and without his finding out that she had taken them.

One night as she was stroking Princess Horrid and the Princess was purring, Pots-and-Pans felt a strange hard knob on top of the kitten's head.

What is that? she wondered, and looked very carefully. It was a tiny gold crown just like the one that the Princess always wore.

"My goodness!" exclaimed Pots-and-Pans. "My kitten is Princess Horrid!"

The Princess could understand everything that was said but could only mew in reply, so she mewed as loudly as she could.

"If you are Princess Horrid, swish your tail about and purr!" ordered Pots-and-Pans. She wanted to be certain that she was right.

Princess Horrid wanted to protest that her name was Hyacinth but, on second thought, decided it was not the right time and place to do so. She swished her tail about violently and purred as loudly as she could.

"You are under a spell." Pots-and-Pans had listened to a great number of fairy tales, so she nodded her head knowingly. "I wonder who cast the spell."

"The Duchess!" Princess Horrid tried to say, but all she could manage was a loud "Miaooow!"

WHEN a week had passed and Princess Horrid had not been found, the King proclaimed that whoever found her would receive a barrel and a half of gold and the title of Supreme Royal Princess Finder. Hardly anyone went to work in the kingdom, they were so busy searching for the Princess.

The Duchess did not join in the hunt, and when anyone asked her why, she merely shrugged her shoulders.

Naturally, Pots-and-Pans, who knew where the Princess was, did not join in the search either. But she asked everyone she knew, and a few people she didn't, how to cure someone who was under a spell. They had all heard about spells and thought that you cast them a bit the way you cast a ball. But as for what to do to someone who was under one, they all pleaded ignorance.

Pots-and-Pans even sneaked into the Royal Library. She was busy scanning all the titles under *S* when the Royal Librarian caught her. He was an old gentleman with a very long beard who spoke eight languages. He held poor Pots-and-Pans by the scruff of the neck and asked her what she was doing.

"Nothing!" she screamed. It was her usual answer to that question.

"Well, go and do nothing somewhere else.... Here one is permitted only to do something!" The Royal Librarian was so pleased with his own joke that he let go of Pots-and-Pans and even offered her a caramel. He was fond of candies and always kept a few in his pockets.

"You would not know, sir," Pots-and-Pans asked timidly, "what should be done for someone who is under a spell?"

"No, I would not." The Royal Librarian popped a caramel into his large mouth, which was shaped like a fish's. "I can spell in eight languages, but I cannot cast a spell in any of them!" The Royal Librarian chuckled and pushed Pots-and-Pans out the door.

THE kitten that was Princess Horrid grew restless in Pots-and-Pans's tiny room. One day, when the door was ajar, she poked her head out. There was no one in sight. She ran quickly up the stairs, leaping from one step to the next. She was just about to run through the South Gallery when the Baroness's white poodle spied her. Princess Horrid ran behind a large oak chest that stood near the wall. The little dog danced and barked around the chest.

"I am Princess Hyacinth," mewed the kitten.

"You are a kitten—and I am going to bite you!" barked the dog, sticking its nose too near Princess Horrid's claws. "Ouch!" it yelped, and ran to its mistress, who had just come in with the rest of the Ladies-in-Waiting.

"Princess Horrid has turned into a cat and she is just as bad as when she was a princess!" yapped the little dog as soon as it was in the Baroness's arms.

"Oh, my poor darling," said the Baroness.

The poodle kept barking to tell her all that had happened, but the Baroness did not know dog language, so she could not understand.

"My poor darling," she said, "has not been so upset since Princess Horrid teased it." At the mention of the Princess all the other ladies joined in, each one outdoing the next in saying what a nasty little girl she had been and how pleased they were that she had disappeared.

"She was a truly horrid brat! She put a slimy toad in my bed," declared the Baroness.

"She put the King's old sock into our soup and itching powder down the poor Chamberlain's back. He was sick for a week!" said another of the Ladies-in-Waiting.

"I hope she will never be found," added a third. "I wouldn't search for her myself for all the gold in the Royal Treasury."

Hiding beneath the chest, Princess Horrid heard it all. At first

she felt proud, as if they had been praising her, but gradually she felt a bit ashamed. I was very childish, she thought as she examined her right paw and pulled her razor-sharp claws in and out.

"She even made an apple-pie bed for the old Duchess," giggled the youngest of the ladies.

"That was brave of her! It is well known that her great-great-grandmother was a witch," said the Baroness.

"The Princess's great-great-grandmother?" asked the young Lady-in-Waiting.

"The Duchess's great-great-grandmother, you goose! She turned the ninth Duke into a poodle and would not turn him back until he promised to marry her. I understand she made him a respectable wife, though. They had nine children."

I had forgotten about that great-great-grandmother. That was a mistake, thought Princess Horrid as she crept silently from the room. I wish I could make her an apple-pie bed right now. Princess Horrid grinned at the thought. It was an extraordinary sight, for it is very seldom you will see a cat grin. Maybe I could make Pots-and-Pans do it for me, she thought as she jumped up on the maid's bed and made herself comfortable. The idea pleased her so much that she purred.

RETURNING from the library, Pots-and-Pans met Fetch-and-Carry, the Duchess's little maid.

"I know what happened to Princess Horrid," said Fetch-and-Carry. "She was turned into a toad and, unless she can make a prince fall in love with her, she will stay a toad forever." Fetch-and-Carry had heard almost as many fairy tales as Pots-and-Pans.

"She is under a spell," Pots-and-Pans agreed. "But who cast it?"

"The Duchess. She is a witch just like her great-great-grandmother. I had to bring her the book of magic. I had decided to run away and not come back after supper, but when she shouted 'Toad!' I got so scared that I ran right then. I wasn't very hungry, anyway." Fetch-and-Carry sniffed.

"Where does she keep the book?" Pots-and-Pans asked eagerly.

"In her bookcase. It is bound in black batskin and has gold edges. It is ever so heavy!" Fetch-and-Carry sighed.

"Thank you!" cried Pots-and-Pans as she started to run back to the castle.

"Now I know who cast the spell and bewitched you!" Pots-and-Pans announced as soon as she had closed the door to her room. "It was the Duchess!"

The Princess opened one eye, stretched herself, and turned over on her back. Finally! she thought. It certainly took her a long time.

"I met Fetch-and-Carry. She told me the Duchess had turned you into a toad."

A toad! Princess Horrid wriggled a little as Pots-and-Pans scratched her tummy. I am glad she didn't turn me into that, she thought.

"She has a book of magic. If we can get hold of it, we might find out how to turn you into a princess again. . . . " But I shall miss my kitten, thought Pots-and-Pans as she spoke.

"Let's make her an apple-pie bed," mewed Princess Horrid as she flexed her claws.

THAT evening the King had a card party. He was fond of games because he always won. For that very reason, the other players at the Royal Card Parties were not so fond of them.

The Duchess had to attend as part of her duties. "What an awful bore!" she told anyone who cared to listen.

Pots-and-Pans put on the better of her two dresses and tied a ribbon in her hair. She felt that if she was going to rob a duchess, she ought to dress for the occasion.

Holding Princess Horrid in her arms, she ran up the stairs of the East Tower. She stopped to listen at the door to the Duchess's apartments, but everything was still. She bent down and looked through the keyhole. There was a faint light, as if a solitary candle was burning.

"I am sure she will turn us into toads if she catches us." Pots-and-Pans opened the door. "But I am not sca—" Half-concealed behind a curtain, a woman was staring at her.

"I am very sorry, ma'am," said Pots-and-Pans quickly. She was just about to run away when she realized that it was a painting hanging on the wall. "Oh, it's only a picture!" Pots-and-Pans laughed to hide her embarrassment. She stepped nearer to have a closer look at the Duchess's great-great-grandmother, and Princess Horrid jumped out of her arms. The old woman certainly looked as if she might have been a champion spell caster in her time.

"I will only borrow your book of magic, ma'am." Pots-and-Pans curtsied to the portrait. The Duchess's great-great-grandmother looked down at her angrily, as if she wanted to turn her into a poodle.

The Duchess's library was not large — two books of fairy tales and the book of magic, which Pots-and-Pans took down from the shelf. It certainly was heavy. She tucked it under her arm and called for the kitten, who was nowhere to be seen.

At last she heard a loud miaow from the next room. It was the Duchess's bedroom. Her bed was a four-poster of carved mahogany, hung with velvet curtains. And there was Princess Horrid, busy tearing at the sheets.

"You naughty kitten!" Pots-and-Pans reached out to pick up the kitten, and suddenly she understood what the kitten wanted her to do.

"You want me to make an apple-pie bed?" she asked.

Princess Horrid purred and swished her tail about.

Pots-and-Pans stripped the blankets and the top sheet from the bed. She tucked the sheet in securely at the head of the bed and doubled it back. She smoothed out a few wrinkles, and there was a perfect apple-pie bed.

Princess Horrid had to admit to herself that Pots-and-Pans was almost as great a master of the art as she was herself.

It was late in the night when the Duchess returned to her chambers.

"Kings," she said, glancing at her great-great-grandmother's portrait, "are an awful bore." As usual, she had lost, and she was a sore loser.

She put on her blue silk nightgown with the diamond buttons. She neither washed nor brushed her teeth. She thought she didn't have to, because she was a duchess.

"Now to bed," she said, and looked wistfully at her four-poster. It was a family heirloom. She jumped into bed and put her feet under...under...

"An apple-pie bed!" she screamed so loudly that a raven who had been dozing peacefully on top of the tower flew away.

"Princess Horrid!" she shouted, and kicked at the sheets. Then she recalled that she had turned the princess into a kitten, and kittens don't make apple-pie beds. "Maybe it was the Baroness," she grumbled as she got up to remake the bed. "If it was, I shall turn her into a toad."

IN her tiny room under the stairs, Pots-and-Pans was busy studying the book of magic. It was late in the night. The candle flickered. It had almost burned down.

"Now I know how to do it!" she exclaimed, waking Princess Horrid, who had been sleeping peacefully. "It is really very simple, Miaow."

Princess Horrid growled. Even though she had been turned into a kitten, she felt that she was still a princess and she did not care for the name she had been given. She put one of her paws up to her head to feel if the crown was still there. It was.

"You have to do everything the opposite way," explained Pots-and-Pans. "If the spell calls for something sour, you put in something sweet. If a plant has to be gathered at midnight, you pluck it at noon instead. It is all under Cure for Spells. ... You will soon be a princess again, Miaow."

"My name is Her Royal Highness Princess Hyacinth!" mewed Princess Horrid as she contemplated her claws. How I shall miss them! she thought, drawing them in and out.

THE very next day, when the Duchess wished to look up a spell for turning the Baroness into a toad, she found that the book of magic was missing.

"Someone in this castle has stolen my book of magic," she complained to the King. "It once belonged to my great-great-grandmother. It was more than a keepsake."

"If it has gone, it might be called a lostsake," suggested the King. He was under the impression that he was witty, for everyone laughed at his jokes, even when they heard them for the tenth time and had not thought them funny the first.

The Duchess did not laugh. As a matter of fact, she frowned. Who could it be? she wondered. The King and Queen were above suspicion. Luckily for Pots-and-Pans, she was below it, for the Duchess had never even heard of her.

"I suspect it was one of the Queen's Ladies-in-Waiting," the Duchess declared.

"Aha," said the King because he did not know what else to say. Suddenly an idea came to him. "Tell me, can you fly on a broomstick?" he asked.

"Certainly not!" The Duchess wanted to add "Blockhead," but it is generally believed unwise to call a king names, so she didn't.

"It would be rather nice if one could." The King looked dreamily at the Duchess, imagining her flying on a broomstick. "Especially on a nice sunny day like today."

"I want my book back!" shouted the Duchess in so command-ing a voice that no one could doubt that she had an admiral and at least three generals among her ancestors.

"If I find it, I will give it to you," the King said mildly. "You might try putting up a notice at the gatehouse offering a reward," he added.

"If I find out who has taken it, I shall reward them, all right," the Duchess muttered grimly as she left. When she was certain that the King could no longer hear her, she shouted "BLOCKHEAD!" in a very loud voice.

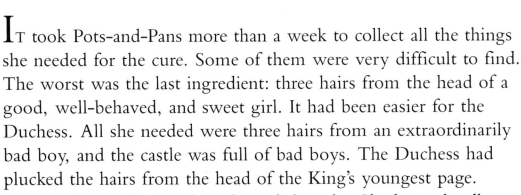

IT took Pots-and-Pans more than a week to collect all the things she needed for the cure. Some of them were very difficult to find. The worst was the last ingredient: three hairs from the head of a good, well-behaved, and sweet girl. It had been easier for the Duchess. All she needed were three hairs from an extraordinarily bad boy, and the castle was full of bad boys. The Duchess had plucked the hairs from the head of the King's youngest page.

Poor Pots-and-Pans thought and thought. She knew hardly any good girls, and certainly none who were both good and well behaved. At last, in desperation, she pulled out three of her own hairs and hoped for the best.

The mixture had to boil for an hour and then cool for two. It smelled strange and unpleasant. But Pots-and-Pans believed that the worse a medicine tasted, the better it was for you.

"It won't taste like cream, Miaow," she said.

"Princess Hyacinth," corrected the kitten, more from habit now than because she cared. I wonder, she thought as she licked her paw in order to wash her face, if it isn't nicer being a cat than a girl, even if you are a princess? You are more comfortable when you sleep, and you have such lovely fur.

When the potion was cool, Pots-and-Pans poured it into a saucer, which it filled to the brim. "Come and drink, Miaow," she called.

Princess Horrid yawned and stretched herself but didn't get up. She could at least call me Princess Miaow, she thought.

"You are a horrid little kitten," Pots-and-Pans wailed. "You don't deserve to be a princess at all!"

Maybe she is right.... Maybe I am horrid, thought the Princess. She got up and arched her back. She jumped off the bed, purred, and rubbed herself against Pots-and-Pans's legs. "If I become a princess again, I think I shall try to be good," she mewed.

"Now drink it." Pots-and-Pans stroked Princess Horrid.

"I can't. It smells horrible," mewed the Princess.

"If you don't drink it, you will have to stay a cat forever," Pots-and-Pans warned.

Princess Horrid stuck out her tongue. It was bright red and more beautiful than any little girl's tongue. She dipped it into the potion. It tasted just as bad as it smelled. It burned like fire in her stomach, but she kept drinking. Since I have started, I might as well finish, she thought, and soon her tongue licked the bottom of the saucer.

Pots-and-Pans watched her drink. "I wonder if it will work," she said aloud. "I did put in the right things and followed the recipe—all but those three hairs from a good and well-behaved girl … but maybe they aren't important." But that is where Pots-and-Pans was wrong. The three hairs were the most important part of the potion.

"Oh, it hurts!" mewed the Princess, and tried to pull her claws in and out. She found that she couldn't, because they were just ordinary fingernails.

Slowly the pain stopped. There she stood, no longer a kitten but Her Royal Highness Princess Hyacinth.

Pots-and-Pans fell on her knees in front of her.

"Arise, Lady…" Princess Hyacinth was just about to say Pots-and-Pans. "Don't you have another name?" she asked.

"I think I did, but I can't remember it. Everyone calls me Pots-and-Pans."

"I shall call you Tulip, and you will be my first Lady-in-Waiting. . . . Arise, Lady Tulip!"

The newly named Lady Tulip rose. Looking down at her reddened hands, she asked, "What does a Lady-in-Waiting do?" She felt certain that at least Ladies-in-Waiting did not scrub pots.

"My mother's only wait around and gossip." Princess Hyacinth laughed. "We'd better go and tell my parents that I am back." She cast one last look around the little room and recalled lying curled up on the bed. "When we are alone, you may call me Miaow," she said, and ran out the door.

Poor Lady Tulip knew that her dress was clean, but that was all that could be said for it. Could she go and see the King and Queen in such rags? Then there was the matter of shoes. She didn't have any. She looked down at her bare toes and wiggled them. They weren't too clean.

"Come along at once!" Princess Hyacinth stuck her head into the room. "It is you—not I—who is supposed to do the waiting!" She had inherited her father's sense of humor.

"SHE has come back!" shouted the Baroness to the other Ladies-in-Waiting.

"Do tell! Do tell!" They twittered like little birds.

"She was under a spell! Turned into a kitten!"

"Who did it? Who did it?"

"The Duchess. She has fled the castle. All the soldiers, the whole army is out looking for her."

At that moment the King and Queen entered, together with Princess Hyacinth and the Supreme Royal Princess Finder, Lady Tulip. The Princess had given Lady Tulip one of her dresses so that she looked respectable. All the ladies curtsied so deeply that they nearly fell.

"My daughter has been under a spell…" the King began, and then stopped. He wasn't very good at making speeches.

"My husband invites you all to a party tonight. There will be two desserts at supper and a grand ball afterward," announced the Queen.

"And fireworks," added Princess Hyacinth. She loved to watch the rockets shoot up into the sky and explode into a mass of stars. "This is my Lady-in-Waiting. She is called Lady Tulip."

She looks like that scullery maid, Pots-and-Pans, thought the Baroness, but she didn't say so aloud until the Royal Family had left.

That is the end of the story. I have told it, and you have heard it. Soon everyone forgot that Princess Hyacinth had ever been called Horrid, or Lady Tulip, Pots-and-Pans. The Duchess was never caught, and to this day the King is certain that she flew away on a broomstick.